Marta Koči

SARAH'S BEAR

PICTURE BOOK STUDIO

WHOO-O-O-O-OOSH!

An enormous wave jumped up
from the sea. It pulled Bear
right off the ship's railing
and into the cold, cold water.

"Help!" he cried. "Bear overboard!"
But nobody heard him. The strong
wind carried his voice away.
Big waves tossed Bear up and down.
They pulled him far, far from
the boat and from the little boy he
belonged to.

Finally the waves tossed him onto a sandy beach.
Poor Bear!
He didn't look much like a teddy bear anymore.
His fur was all wet and tangled, and he had even
lost his ears.

He had not been there very long before someone
found him. It was a little girl named Sarah.
Sarah and her dog had been fishing.
"Oh, look!" she cried.
"This poor little bear must have fallen off someone's boat.
He looks half-drowned. Let's take him home with us."
Sarah was always bringing home animals that needed
to be loved and cared for.

Now Sarah walked home
from the beach, carrying
Bear very gently. As they
walked past the village,
she talked to him softly.
"Don't be afraid, little bear,"
she said. But Bear was afraid.
Where was she taking him?
Would he ever see his home
again, and the little boy who
owned him? The little boy
had never been very nice to him,
in fact, but now Bear was so
lonely he missed him. But the
sun was warm, and Bear was tired,
and soon he drifted off to sleep.

"Here we are – we're home!" said Sarah.
Bear opened his eyes in surprise.

"This is Bear," said Sarah to the others. "He's going to live with us."

Sarah lived in a house with Cat, Dog, Crow, Goat, Goose-and-her-little-goslings, and Pig. Pig was very kind. She did the cooking and looked after the others whenever Sarah was gone. The house was a little crowded because of all the animals that Sarah had brought to live in it, but it was tidy and pleasant.

"Bear's a sailor, who's travelled a long way and had many exciting adventures," Sarah said. "He can tell us lots of stories as soon as he feels better."

Everyone helped Sarah take care of Bear. Sarah bathed him in warm water and dried him with a fluffy towel. She sewed up the little places that had been torn in the rough sea. He still didn't look much like a bear, as Sarah couldn't replace his ears. But he found that he could hear without them, and everyone liked him just as he was. Bear had never had friends before. It gave him a warm feeling inside, and the corners of his mouth turned up in a shy smile.

"Let's have a party for Bear," suggested Crow one day.
"Oh, yes, let's," gabbled Goose. She loved parties.

"I'll go to market and get something nice for the party,"
 said Pig. "I'll take Bear with me."
 Carefully, she picked him up.
"I'll come, too," said Crow.
"Me, too," barked Dog.

Soon they had all the food they would need.
"Now, how about some sweets, please," begged Dog.
"Well, just this once," said Pig, as she always did.
Dog sat down beside Bear while they ate their treats.
"I'm glad you came to live with us, Bear," he said.

What a wonderful party they had! Bear, who was the guest of honor, sat with Sarah. After all had eaten their fill of the good food, Bear told the others many stories of his adventures at sea.

Then the whole family gathered under the
tree in front of the house to watch the sunset.
Sarah held Bear in her arm. At her feet,
Dog stretched out and closed his eyes.
It was a quiet, peaceful time.
Bear felt a special warmth inside.

"It's funny," said Bear. "I don't seem to
want to go home anymore after all."
"Oh, Bear," said Sarah. "You *are* home."

"Bedtime, everyone," called Pig.

And soon Bear and Sarah
and all their good friends
were sound asleep and dreaming
happily of tomorrow's adventures.
Through the open window,
the moon looked in
and seemed to smile.

A Michael Neugebauer Book
Copyright © 1987, Neugebauer Press, Salzburg, Austria.
Published and distributed in USA by Picture Book Studio, Saxonville, MA.
Distributed in Canada by Vanwell Publishing, St. Catharines, Ont.
Published in UK by Picture Book Studio, Neugebauer Press Ltd., London.
Distributed in UK by Ragged Bears, Andover.
Distributed in Australia by Era Publications, Adelaide.
All rights reserved.
Printed in Hong Kong.

LIBRARY OF CONGRESS CATALOGING IN PUBLICATION DATA
Koči, Marta.
Sarah's bear.
Summary: The adventures of a teddy bear who, after a wave sweeps him
off a big ship, is found on an island beach by a little girl named Sarah.
[1. Teddy bears – Fiction. 2. Islands – Fiction] I. Title.
PZ7.K8174Sar   1987   [E]   86-30241
ISBN 0-88708-038-3

Ask your bookseller for these other PICTURE BOOK STUDIO books by Marta Koci:
BLACKIE & MARIE
KATIE'S KITTEN

E
YOL

Yolen, Jane.

The day Tiger Rose
said goodbye.

Grades K-3

$16.99

11-0915

DATE			

To the memory of Amber Dextrose, Pod, Colin, Nuncle, Penny Dreadful,
and Math vab Mathonwy—best of cats, best of friends
—J.Y.

Text copyright © 2011 by Jane Yolen
Jacket art and interior illustrations copyright © 2011 by Jim LaMarche

Visit us on the Web! www.randomhouse.com/kids

Educators and librarians, for a variety of teaching tools, visit us at www.randomhouse.com/teachers

Library of Congress Cataloging-in-Publication Data
Yolen, Jane.
The day Tiger Rose said goodbye / Jane Yolen ; illustrations by Jim LaMarche. — 1st ed.
p. cm.
Summary: A cat whose kitten days are far behind her says goodbye to her human family, and the
animals and places that have made her life special, before leaving this life behind.
ISBN 978-0-375-86663-0 (trade) — ISBN 978-0-375-96663-7 (lib. bdg.)
[1. Cats—Fiction. 2. Death—Fiction. 3. Country life—Fiction.] I. LaMarche, Jim, ill. II. Title.
PZ7.Y78 Day 2011
[E]—dc22
2010013548

MANUFACTURED IN CHINA

10 9 8 7 6 5 4 3 2 1

First Edition

11-0915
WILLIMANTIC PUBLIC LIBRARY
CHILDREN'S DEPARTMENT

The Day Tiger Rose
Said Goodbye

By Jane Yolen
Illustrated by Jim LaMarche

RANDOM HOUSE 🏠 NEW YORK

The day Tiger Rose said goodbye

was a soft spring day,

the sun only half risen.

Little brilliant butterflies,

like bits of colored paper,

floated among the flowers.

Tiger Rose had been born in the city,

but now she lived in the country

in a house filled with laughter and cat treats.

There, a boy and a girl loved her,

a dog named Rowf tolerated her,

and two grown-ups called Mom and Pop

let her sit on the sofa

as long as she did not use her claws.

But Tiger Rose was tired now

and she had gotten slow,

her kitten days so long ago

they were only small sparks of memory,

as fleeting as the butterflies.

Her back legs sometimes hurt

and she had a ringing in her ears.

She no longer had an appetite for chasing food.

Tiger Rose was getting ready to say goodbye.

High in the pine a solitary jay scolded,

"Do not come here, Tiger Rose.

Do not come here."

Rowf slept on the first step of the house,

nose on brindle paws.

"It is time," Tiger Rose said to the jay,

to the butterflies,

to Rowf, deep in a doggy dream.

She knew they did not listen to her

but she said it anyway.

It brought her comfort.

She meowed goodbye to Mom and Pop first

as they headed off in their cars,

though they barely noticed her.

She said farewell to the boy and girl

walking to school.

The girl stopped and gave Tiger Rose

a tickle under the chin,

as if she knew something was about to happen.

"Be easy," the girl whispered. "I'll remember."

Tiger Rose went to the bushes then

and said her goodbyes to them,

old friends, old shade.

Next she sniffed the green thrusts beneath the pine,

which smelled fresh and new, like kittens.

Tiger Rose touched noses with the moles and voles

and a chipmunk by the stone wall,

all of whom were surprised at her gentleness.

The little snake who lived behind the barn
startled and stopped slithering to look at her,
but did not speak except for a low hiss.
"It is time," Tiger Rose told him. "Goodbye."
She looked up at the nest of starlings under the eaves
and didn't even mind their squawkings.
"Goodbye," she whispered.
It sounded like a purr.

She stepped over anthills,

careful not to tread on any ants,

and walked slowly under an arch of azalea boughs.

With her tail, she saluted

the hive of bees behind the house

as they buzzed about their business.

Her purr was louder now.

At the feeders on the porch,

she said goodbye to a pair of buff-colored sparrows,

and to four goldfinches

who looked like a bit of flying sunlight.

"Goodbye. Goodbye."

At last, Tiger Rose sat down

to clean herself from head to tail.

When she was done, she stood and stretched,

making an arch of her striped back.

Clouds scudded across the sky,

flinging themselves

from one end of the blue to the other.

A stray wind puzzled through the trees.

The butterflies flitted from flower to flower

without speaking, without stopping

for longer than a moment or two.

Everything was either quick or dreaming,

but not Tiger Rose.

"It is time," Tiger Rose said again,

but now just to herself.

She lay down under the rosebushes,

heavy with early buds.

There she curled into a soft ball.

Closing her eyes, she envisioned

gathering for one last jump,

landing on a thin span of sun.

Then she walked slowly up and up and up,

past moles and voles,

chipmunks and snakes,

past the house,

where Rowf still drowsed,

past the blossoming azalea,

past the top of the pine,

past the scudding clouds,

and into the luminous blue sky.

She never once looked back

as she climbed away from life,

leaving her old and tired body behind.

Up and up and up she went,

and then she was gone,

now part of the earth, the air, the sky, the sun —

and all.